FLANNERY O'CONNOR'S CHARACTERS

Laurence Enjolras

University Press of America,® Inc.
Lanham • New York • Oxford

University Press of America,® Inc.
4720 Boston Way
Lanham, Maryland 20706

12 Hid's Copse Rd.
Cummor Hill, Oxford OX2 9JJ

Printed in the United States of America
British Library Cataloging in Publication Information Available

Library of Congress Cataloging-in-Publication Data

Enjolras, Laurence.
Flannery O'Connor's characters / Laurence Enjolras.
p. cm.
Includes bibliographical references.
1. O'Connor, Flannery—Characters. 2. Characters and characteristics in literature. 3. Southern States—In literature. I. Title.
PS3565.C57Z6655 1998 813'.54—DC21 97-53102 CIP

ISBN 978-0-7618-1040-7

™ The paper used in this publication meets the minimum requirements of American National Standard for information Sciences—Permanence of Paper for Printed Library Materials, ANSI Z39.48—1984

Ricky pour mémoire

CONTENTS

ACKNOWLEDGMENTS

I would like to thank the Committee on Fellowships, Research and Publication at the College of the Holy Cross for granting me funds for this project.

Et toi, Lanny, pour ce qu'il advint de ces pages.

NOTE

The present study is only taking into account Flannery O'Connor's short stories. The textbook referred to is:

O'Connor, Flannery. *The Complete Stories*. New York: Farrar, Straus & Giroux, 1971.

Some of the stories contained in this collected edition, which, revised or expanded, became chapters of Flannery O'Connor's two novel, have not been considered. They are:

"The Train."
"The Peeler."
"The Heart of the Park."
"Enoch and the Gorilla."
"You Can't Be Any Poorer Than Dead."

INTRODUCTION

Mary Flannery O'Connor spent most of her adult life with her mother on a dairy farm just outside Milledgeville, Georgia, after she was hit with disseminated lupus, an incurable disease that forced her into an involuntary isolation. It is often considered that this isolation greatly constricted her range of topics, as indeed her fiction abounds with settings and themes pertaining to southern country life, and for the most part, deals with rustic characters. The humorous tone with which she tells the difficulties of her protagonists, all Protestants, in recognizing their religious beliefs and in handling their encounters with God might mislead careless readers into believing that all she did in her short stories was mock the Protestant faith and deride the backwoods individuals who rove the desolate, unfriendly clay roads of her fictional world.

Flannery O'Connor's answer to such an erroneous interpretation of her work was vehement. In numerous lectures and articles, she explained her role and intentions as a fiction writer, seeing herself as a prophet with a warning and a message to deliver to her readers. Above all, she made clear that she saw everything from the standpoint of Christian orthodoxy. Born a Roman Catholic and a Southerner, she always insisted that these two peculiarities, far from being a hindrance to her as a writer, put her instead in a privileged situation. Concerned with realism as she was, the country she felt she could depict in the most objective way was, of course, the region she knew best because she had lived there the majority of her life: the South. It is the South which constitutes the main ground of her stories, depicted with its regional characteristics, its specific body of manners, its idioms and speech rhythm, in other words, with all the particulars which create the powerful image of its strong and unique identity. The South O'Connor describes is what is called the Bible Belt, a region where the Bible is known to everyone, where religious themes find a response in the life of the people, where Protestant believers wrestle with their faith in all kinds of dramatic ways, or simply fail to recognize the nature of a religious desire burning inside of them. As a writer concerned with religious themes, Flannery O'Connor felt that the South offered her a particularly suitable ground of observation.

As a Roman Catholic, the author expresses her own religious convictions and her personal vision of life in clearly defined terms. She believes that life has been given by God to be worth dying for, knows that the universe is meaningful, recognizes sin as an offense against God, accepts evil as a mystery which man has to endure and to which he is prone, sees man as incomplete in himself, as an insignificant being unable to manage by himself, thus having to seek God's help and guidance to enlighten his life. However, O'Connor's ultimate vision is one of hope because she believes in Redemption, in God's generous Will to love and to forgive, in divine grace bestowed to those who humbly ask for it.

In her fiction, Flannery O'Connor undertook to dramatize her indictment of the materialism, the secularism, and the liberal optimism of contemporary life. Condemning human pharisaism, she wanted to restore in the mind of her readers that sense of "evil" and "good" she felt was much blurred, even forgotten, and to demonstrate the necessity of a supernatural assistance. Knowing that for the most part her audience would be hostile and that the number of Catholics reading her works would be limited, she was particularly conscious of the necessity to create a fiction which had to stand out on its own, to be both self-explanatory and cogent. She created characters whom she presented at a turning point in their life. Children, adolescents or adults, her protagonists are shown floundering in a petty universe in which their sinful nature tends to overwhelm their indefinite sense of the vast importance of a salvation they cannot clearly grasp. But she captures them at the moment when they are offered the opportunity to rid themselves of their religious blindfolds and, having done so, to respond to divine grace.

In the following chapters, we shall analyze some recurrent character types O'Connor presented in her fiction and the way she delivered her message through the violently illuminating experiences her protagonists live through. In preparation for this, however, it is important to reflect on the physical appearance of characters, whom she portrayed almost exclusively as distorted, maimed and ugly. Doing so, she obviously intended to proclaim and emphasize the intrinsic imperfection of man as opposed to the divine perfection of God.

CHAPTER 1

PHYSICAL PORTRAIT: THE UGLY HUMAN BODY

In the opening piece of *Mystery and Manners* entitled "The King of the Birds," we are startled yet not really amazed to learn that, still a child but already passionate about raising fowl, Flannery O'Connor "favored those with one green eye and one orange or with overlong necks and crooked combs," and above all, "wanted one with three legs or three wings."[1] Such oddity can only bring back to the mind of the readers of her fiction similar peculiarities which many of her characters are afflicted with. Read separately or as a whole, her short stories strike first with unforgettably distorted, mutilated or maimed bodies craftily depicting a vivid but frightening world — and yet, at times, a strangely comical one — in which many of the protagonists seem to have come straight out of the asylum.

To the average reader unaccustomed to encountering such types of characters, the blatant grotesques of

O'Connor's picture is somewhat repulsive. Her vision of life so exclusively manifests itself through freaks that if we let ourselves be impressed by her very personal and highly peculiar conception of the world, we soon come to wonder whether there is any hope left of ever seeing beauty around us again. In fact, Flannery O'Connor was often asked why she delighted so much at portraying grotesque characters. She felt this to be a misconception on the part of her readers and often endeavored to eradicate so regrettable a misunderstanding, both in lectures and in articles about literature. She remarked:

> I have written several stories which did not seem to me to have any grotesque characters in them at all, but which have immediately been labeled grotesque by non-Southern readers.[2]
>
> Even though the writer who produces grotesque fiction may not consider his characters any more freakish than ordinary fallen man usually is, his audience is going to; and it is going to ask him — or more often, tell him — why he has chosen to bring such maimed souls alive.[3]

In these lines O'Connor asserts that her characters are nothing more than ordinary people who can be seen and met in reality. She stated repeatedly that a fiction writer writes indeed about what he can observe around him in plain everyday life: "What-is is all he has to do with; the concrete is his medium."[4]

However, she knew that her vision of "what-is," of "ordinary fallen man," would strike many of her readers as anything but ordinary, and for them would be difficult to accept and almost certainly impossible to share. In addition, she felt that some might not even perceive the prophecies contained in her stories. She thus explained and justified her strange characters as well as the means by which she made her message tangible:

> you have to make your vision apparent by shock — to the hard of hearing you shout, and for the almost-blind you draw large and startling figures.[5]

Startling indeed are the figures which appear before us. As we go through the stories, we have the impression that we are moving inside a gallery whose walls have been covered with deforming mirrors which reflect grinning faces and distorted bodies of all shapes and dimensions. As a matter of fact, we do not confront human beings; we encounter monsters who assail us either with their defects, with their impairments, or with their clownishness, caught as they are — fierce, violent, pathetic creatures — in the gruesome show of the puppet life through which they totter. The pictures could easily turn into nightmares as scenes come to life not so much with people as with ghastly substitutes: Joy-Hulga fundamentally *is* her wooden-leg ("Good Country People"), Rufus Johnson his club-foot ("The Lame Shall Enter First"), General Sash his wheelchair ("A Late Encounter with the Enemy"), Mr. Shiftlet his missing forearm ("The Life You Save May Be Your Own"), while the background glints with the sparks of dental braces or metallic curlers. Such a fascination with the macabre on the part of the author brings back to mind that cynical comment of hers upon her return from a pilgrimage to Lourdes, France: "I had the best looking crutches in Europe."[6] When they are not crippled, her characters still appear as caricatures, so that it is clear that for O'Connor, the human body is essentially deprived of dignity or respectability. In no instance is it ever granted beauty. In

"The Displaced Person," when, surprised and pleased for the first time, we read the description of young Sledgewig Guizac as a nice little girl with "long braided hair in two looped pigtails" about whom "there was no denying she was a pretty child," (p. 197) the charming image is but a fleeting one, shadowed by Mrs. Shortley's caustic remark that the little girl's name sounds "like something you would name a bug, or vice versa." (p. 195) Powerful descriptions of that nature have a tendency to gradually and slyly set into readers' mind as they get more and more familiar with Flannery O'Connor's strange world. In the present instance, it is not long before we realize with shock that we have been influenced by the author's artful devices as if by a contagious disease, and that we in turn have slowly come to think of the little girl as a bug.

Most of the bodies of O'Connor's characters are ugly, repulsive, sorry, or defective and have to rely on all kinds of plastic or metallic artificial aids in order to remain functional. However, instead of lessening the deformities they are supposed to correct, these devices only serve to magnify them; most importantly, they take such a role and have such an impact on the personality of their unfortunate users that they become the only major concrete means by which they can define themselves, shaping their identity, becoming their essence, and finally dominating their lives. The body is thus trapped, shown like a rickety hindrance, condemned as something to loathe.

In keeping with the tradition of the grotesque, Flannery O'Connor's portraits picture human beings in terms of animal imagery, fixing the characters in fantastic, despicable attitudes. Comparisons with the monkey, the bear, the frog, the sheep, the goat, the spider, the bulldog abound, evoked in the least flattering of positions: they squat, wait while passively chewing, scowl, frown, or simply keep motionless, stupid, and dumb. In her many comparisons with insects, O'Connor uses the only one which might have been poetical because of the naturally colorful gracefulness and ethereal lightness associated with it — the butterfly — in such an ominous way that the readers' expectations are very quickly inverted and their associations immediately channeled into the bleak spheres in which reigns the gloomy moth. Indeed, our craving for beauty is met with disappointment when we read that

> a fluttering figure had begun to move forward with a kind of butterfly movement — an old woman with flapping arms whose head wobbled as if it might fall off any second. (p. 166)

With this sharp and deft sentence, O'Connor forbids the way to dreams. Her remorseless attack on her readers' aesthetic sensibility gradually takes oppressive dimensions and aims at conveying an increasing uneasiness before a world she forces us to regard as the norm: it is but a haunting society teeming with insidious individuals adorned with blank, cabbage-like faces, who flounder in a hostile, evil environment.

Shock and stupor seize the reader with every new detail Flannery O'Connor unleashes to sketch out the physical portraits of her protagonists. Significantly, they present extreme characteristics, invariably graceless. Either fat, plump, stout, stocky, solidly planted on tremendous limbs, set like mountains with bulging stomachs and mammoth bosoms, squeezed and packed in their clothes to offer the image of tubular bundles; or bony, dried and shriveled in dead chicken skin, gaunt, frail, sour and puckered like rotten apples; all of them, children included, carry around the sorry look of old age and stroll about with the staggering gait of those whose condition is a helpless mystery to themselves in spite of their being convinced that they can see clearly through the events of their lives. In addition, several characters are mutilated: one is missing a leg, another an arm, a third one a good foot. To put the finishing touch to this sinister sketch-book, a cripple is wheeled around in his chair, an idiot child is abused, a hermaphrodite exhibits his misfortune in a circus.

If the general appearance of the characters is shabby and sad enough, the details of their faces or bodies when focused on are even worse. Flannery O'Connor seems to revel in gruesome afflictions. It is as if she had banished forever the word "handsome" from her mind and vocabulary. The seedy-looking figures we are introduced to are topped with the most wretched faces which constitute an unforgettable portrait gallery, and which, at times, remind us of some of Goya's hideously distorted paintings. The features are ominous, either when crinkled, parched skin hangs down on protruding bones, or when they set in harmless innocent expressions on the florid, puffy, moon-like, baby-smooth faces of some characters. All shades of colors, ranging from the palest white to the ugliest red, muddy yellow to acne blue, blend in their complexion. Scattered here and there, a fair share of warts, spots, lumps, bulges, and the like combine with ears which often take enormous dimensions, are shaped like a pig's or a rabbit's, or twitch convulsively. Skulls, when they are not bright, rosy, and bald, seem to be wigged with preposterous puffs of uncontrollable hair darting in every direction if they have not been momentarily tamed and set in sausage rolls by plastic or metallic curlers, or else stuffed under rags used as head-kerchiefs; yellow, peroxided, whitish, gray, tobacco-colored, black, either slicked back and greasy or stuck with sweat, the hair certainly never constitutes an adornment;

rather, it resembles these other bizarre extremities of the body: feet which dangle and fat hands which hang helplessly.

In the very same vein, mouths never smile; they invariably grin, opening on black caverns one suspects to be nauseating, planted here and there with long yellow teeth or rotten stubs which delimit gaps of irregular sizes on collapsing gums; they stretch, revealing the metallic glare of braces; they drop open, disclosing rigid tongues erecting from a pool of slobber; or again, completely toothless, they gape, sucking in to outline a cutting profile. So that the final vision of the characters' uncomely expressions is a very acid one indeed, increased by the weirdness of their gaze, which seems to keep us under a spell. Unsettled by the quizzical look of beady eyes or by the blurred stare of an old Negro whose eyes "seemed to be hung behind cobwebs," (p. 215) we remain disturbed long after we have finished reading the stories by the numerous twists and blemishes that impair eyes which otherwise glare with a devilish or supernatural light. More than any other part of the faces or bodies, the eyes seem to exist and function as perfectly independent units, in mismatched pairs: out of the two, one is listing toward the outer rim; one is more nearly round than the other; one draws near to the other; one is stuck; one is blind; one is almost rolling out of the head; one has a slight cast to it; one is twisted inward; one is moving to the left while the other is fixed; one is bloodshot. Indeed, the list of impairments is endless. But eyes have one common characteristic: they remain unfathomable, as impossible to meet and actually establish some kind of contact with as those which, crossed, near-sighted, shifty, or simply defective, shelter behind the thickest of glasses.

Despite such disparity and disharmony, the portraits prove to be drawn along classical lines, as

O'Connor generally respects the traditional symbolism of colors: the innocent have blue eyes whereas the mischievous exhibit dark ones. In her essay entitled "The Church and the Fiction Writer," O'Connor explains:

> For the writer of fiction, everything has its testing point in the eye, an organ which eventually involves the whole personality and as much of the world as can be got into it. Msgr. Romano Guardini has written that the roots of the eye are in the heart.[7]

Such a statement is well illustrated in her characters: innocent Lucynell ("The Life You Save May Be Your Own"), generous Sheppard ("The Lame Shall Enter First"), candid Claud ("Revelation"), honest Thomas ("The Comforts of Home"), or irresponsible Norton ("The Lame Shall Enter First") cast clear, pale blue glances around them; whereas suspicious Mrs. Cope ("A Circle in the Fire"), tormented Misfit ("A Good Man Is Hard to Find"), unbalanced Singleton ("The Partridge Festival"), or puzzling Mr. Shiftlet ("The Life You Save May Be Your Own") express the mysterious worries which haunt them in the frowning look of their dark-colored eyes. Ultimately, the eyes embody the very essence of the characters, as vexed Mrs. Shortley demonstrates when she curtly comments about Mr. Guizac, The Displaced Person: "It's them little eyes of his that's foreign." (p. 206) Significantly, many of the characters wear spectacles, as if, Sister M. Bernetta Quinn points out, "to extend sight beyond the ordinary,"[8] at least, to add to the otherwise large collection of orthopaedic aids without which they would not be able to function.

Considered from a distance, set in their crooked positions, trapped by their crippled bodies, sometimes even buried alive in their defective flesh, diseased, impaired, or dislocated in a grotesque manner, the characters of these stories do try over and over to convey a message, and indeed we must consider Flannery O'Connor's repeated use of such hideous details as a technical device which focuses on and emphasizes the fundamental imperfection of the human body. Perfection on earth is impossible to find, she tells us, and evil is present everywhere, is part of our reality. Thus, we should not grant any importance to anything earthly, rather, we should endeavor to look beyond our immediate surroundings. As ugly and defective as it may be, the human body should be accepted just the way it is, even if it becomes the worst of oppressors. Incidentally, let us not forget that O'Connor herself suffered much from the disease she contracted, although she always kept her self-control behind her scornful humor and sarcastic comments, nor should we overlook the fact that "she took a sardonic pleasure in being photographed, grim and unsmiling, against the unpainted and dilapidated house of their Negro tenant farmers."[9]

Many of her protagonists meet physically violent deaths: Mrs. May gets gored by a bull ("Greenleaf"); Tanner dies stuck between the spokes of a banister and must be sawn out ("Judgement Day"); Mary Fortune and her grandfather beat each other to death with violent rage ("A View of the Woods"); Mr. Guizac is run over by a tractor ("The Displaced Person"). However shocking and disturbing such physical tortures may appear to average readers, Flannery O'Connor invites us to consider what deeper implications the deaths of her protagonists carry. As she has explained, death is that moment when divine grace has been offered, when the characters have been redeemed:

> in my own stories I have found that violence is strangely capable of returning my characters to reality and preparing them to accept their moment of grace.[10]

Of course, we are to understand that O'Connor sees a gap between body and mind, that those cannot and never will meet. In fact, none of her characters seem to have both a functioning mind and a functioning body at the same time. Besides, the bodies escape any kind of control from their possessors; rather, they are the ones to have control, playing tricks on them. Even though she claimed to have shown reality, O'Connor was well aware that reality might be different for different people, and that the situations she was making alive in her work was one that many ordinary people would never be given to observe, let alone experience during their lives. She chose to make her vision more tangible by using violent and shocking imagery, for she was convinced that only if her readers were shaken could she be heard:

> Distortion in this case is an instrument; exaggeration has a purpose, and the whole structure of the story or novel has been made what it is because of belief. This is not the kind of distortion that destroys; it is the kind that reveals, or should reveal.[11]

This artistic device proves to be a powerful one indeed, for the author manages to upset us with such characters. After having analyzed the way O'Connor enhances the imperfection of the human body, we shall consider how she deals with the imperfection of the human being.

CHAPTER 2

WICKED CHILDREN

In the long essay she wrote as an introduction to *A Memoir of Mary Ann*, Flannery O'Connor stated in her usual decisive tone that "[b]ad children are harder to endure than good ones, but they are easier to read about,"[1] a statement which readers of her fiction are at once tempted to enlarge, adding that not only are they easier to read about, but most certainly they seem easier to write about. Out of the twenty-six short stories dealt with in this study of her fiction, sixteen of them show children whom the author did not contrive to depict as virtuous but rather endeavored to paint with whatever evil she could see in them, either in speech, thought, or action. "Stories of pious children tend to be false," she wrote in the essay quoted above, and she further explained why:

> This may be because they are told by adults, who see virtue where their subjects would see only a practical course of action; or it may be because

> such stories are written to edify and what is written to edify usually ends by amusing. (p. 213)

Even though her treatment of children may take comical dimensions because of certain situations and above all because of her gift to render folk speech and the often disarming spontaneity of children's wit, O'Connor's stories are far from being merely amusing. Little by little, as each one unfolds, we come to realize that in most cases, the children are intrigued by an impervious mystery, then coerced by a force which they sense as being imperious, one which they cannot really understand nor identify, thus leaving them confused.

Of course, we must distinguish between the children who are minor characters, only displaying some kind of mischievous behavior — albeit realistically and craftily rendered — from the ones whose deeds take deeper and devilish tinges, shaking our confident naïveté, often bringing us to face horror because of their violence, leaving us positively aghast. Flannery O'Connor rejects and disrupts the romantic world of fictional tales which shines with the image of little girls and boys as sweet models of graciousness and kindness. The children she depicts are sullen, ill-tempered, rude, selfish, violent, insubordinate, mean, obdurate, grim. In fact, they too are trapped in a world in which evil reigns; they too have to suffer from it; they too have to live the frustration and the ordeal until they have grown enough to be able to grasp the meaning of it and understand that "evil is not simply a problem to be solved, but a mystery to be endured."[2]

However, it gives the world O'Connor presents a quality and an oddity which may leave many a reader skeptical when some of the children she allots with either religious fanaticism or blind faith meet tragic or violent deaths because of their religiosity.

It should be remarked that not all the children of the stories directly illustrate the personal religious convictions which Flannery O'Connor interweaves through the personalities of her different characters. In fact, some of them do not at all. Nonetheless, they are interesting because of the very fine moral portraits the author manages to sketch, portraits which are strikingly realistic and precise. Such are June Star and John Wesley in "A Good Man Is Hard to Find," Joanne and Susan in "A Temple of the Holy Ghost," Mrs. Connin's three sons in "The River," or Hartley Gilfeet in "A Stroke of Good Fortune"; in these children, sin manifests itself in its venial aspect: they quarrel with each other, play tricks on one another, giggle in fits of mockery, use foul or even rude language to address their relatives and neighbors. Because of their childish egotism, they remain oblivious of respect or simple care for others and are little or not aware of the mysterious presence and power of a God whom they seem hardly concerned with in spite of the many hints given to them — and which clearly do not succeed in provoking any kind of response on their part. The healing at the river ("The River") or the spirit of the convent ("A Temple of the Holy Ghost") do not seem to carry any deeper implication in the minds of the young, thoughtless children involved; similarly, the religious talks or Christian behavior we assume the grandmother to have conformed to during her life ("A Good Man Is Hard to Find") do not seem to have influenced her heedless grandchildren much. What Flannery O'Connor shows us in these instances is a rather unpleasant group of noisy and dull children whose concerns are low, whose religious fervor is null, who are not particularly striking in themselves, but who are realistically perceived as tiresome or vain.

In contrast, other children have something intriguing about them that, in some cases, will become even appalling or horrifying. Let us first consider Nelson, the protagonist of "The Artificial Nigger" and Mary Fortune Pitts, the protagonist of "A View of the Woods." Both are afflicted with the same failing: pride; both are used by the author in the same way in stories that are parallel in their aim at demonstrating the eventual collapse and ultimate failure of people eaten up by such a penchant. Even though both grandfathers in the two stories are considered as the main characters, Nelson and Mary Fortune are also important inasmuch as they too are given the possibility to learn a lesson of humility, whether they choose to recognize it, as Nelson does, or refuse to accept it, as Mary Fortune will. The denouement is the point where the two stories diverge: whereas Nelson and his grandfather, each at his own level, have been led to wisdom through the revelation of what forgiveness means and to their entry into a world newly charged for them with the grandeur of God, Mary Fortune, who has repeated over and over the menacing phrase: "[n]obody's ever beat me in my life . . . and if anybody did, I'd kill him," (p. 351) refuses to let the justly aroused wrath of her grandfather fall upon her, proceeds to kick and to beat the old man, then dies in the middle of a raging fit of fierce stubbornness which Mr. Fortune puts to an end when he knocks her head against a rock which happens to protrude from the clay. Without really knowing what was happening, Nelson sensed that some important chance was given to him and he seized it intuitively; in contrast, by denying out of pure pride the punishment that her misconduct deserved, Mary Fortune missed the hint for which she was not yet ready. As Sister Kathleen Feeley establishes in her study entitled *Flannery O'Connor: Voice of the Peacock*:

> In the course of the action, all characters are given an opportunity to recognize their self-deception. In the author's vision, this recognition is the first step toward truth, which is, in turn, the necessary condition of Redemption. Conversion — a change of direction — is possible only after one recognizes his perversion.[3]

In that sense, Nelson differs greatly from the children mentioned earlier inasmuch as coming across a situation in which he is given the opportunity to correct his pride, he does react in the right way, if only out of intuition. As for Mary Fortune, she too differs greatly from them inasmuch as her behavior is not childish mischief anymore but horrifying violence bursting as an uncontrolled force emerging from a passionate nature unleashing pure hatred.

Puzzling and unexpected, behaving in ways rarely seen among children their age, are Powell and his two friends Garfield Smith and W.T. Harper, three urchins from the city who invade Mrs. Cope's farm and gradually haunt the whole place with their undesired and harassing presence until they manage in a final culminating act of irresponsibility to set fire to Mrs. Cope's precious woods ("A Circle in the Fire"). From their first appearance occurring at the close of a vapid conversation between Mrs. Pritchard and Mrs. Cope, in which the latter asserts with confidence that she feels ready to encounter whatever misery might turn up, there is something ominous about them which becomes more and more alarming as they vanish out of sight, being then regularly reported on by the hired help at every one of their malevolent interventions; so that the more we progress into the story, the more they are perceived as an increasing threat, and ultimately as an ineluctable one. As in the two tales mentioned earlier, Powell and his friends are secondary characters in a story where the focus is put on Mrs. Cope's downfall. But they do have a dimension and role of their own: they represent the symbolic intuition and longing for a paradisiac world, a world better than the tangible reality which surrounds them. Powell, who remembers what happy days he spent on the farm in his youth — his family once lived there as hired help — drags his two friends in his quest for a lost Eden, the image of which has been haunting him ever since he has been living in "one of them developments" (p. 179) out in Atlanta. As W.T. Harper explains to the two ladies, Powell "[s]aid it was everything there. . . . Said he had the best time of his entire life right here on this here place. Talks about it all the time." (p. 180) Most importantly, he once "said when he died he wanted to come here," (p. 180) indicating that the farm represents not only a paradise in which to live one's life, but also and above all a paradise in which to rest in peace and joy after death, and a paradise which all three acknowledge to be God's as they retort to Hollis Pritchard coming to reprimand them: "Gawd owns them woods and her [Mrs. Cope] too." (p. 186) However, the resentment towards God we had sensed in their muteness after Mrs. Cope's inquiries about their thanking God "for everything" is ultimately turned into a violent fit of passion as they set out to destroy and burn the paradise which they cannot fully enjoy, convinced that "[if] this place was not here any more . . . [they] would never have to think of it again." (p. 192) This act of destruction which aims at annihilating an obsessing but unattainable heaven symbolically represents the inability of human beings to understand God's will and to wait until the time He appoints. Powell and his friends do exhibit a certain religious intuition but one which is tragically immature. They rebel because the frustration they must live through is an ordeal they comprehend only in secular terms, that is to say, not at all.

When we turn to Ruller, the protagonist of "The Turkey," Harry, the protagonist of "The River," or the young girl who appears in "A Temple of the Holy Ghost," as well as Rufus Johnson, the young fanatic of "The Lame Shall Enter First," Martha Stephens's assertion that Flannery O'Connor

> never endowed any of her grown children with true Christian belief, although, like nearly all her protagonists, they are usually closer to some kind of religious understanding or belief at the end of their harrowing tales than they are in the beginning[4]

takes its full dimension. Indeed, each of these children has more than the vague intuition of God that the children previously mentioned exhibit; they have a consciousness of Him which, by the end of the stories, has developed into a strong certainty of His Presence and Power, even though they cannot account for it with full lucidity. In "The Turkey," we follow the conversion of young Ruller from a state of inconsiderate impiety ("God," "God dammit," "God dammit to hell," "Our Father Who art in heaven, shoot 'em six and roll 'em seven," p. 46) into a fit of overwhelming confidence in which he feels suddenly that "God must be wonderful. . . . He wanted to do something for God. . . . He had never thought before of praying on his own, but it was a good idea," (p. 51) convinced that he has been selected by God to be a preacher or to "found a place for boys to stay who were going bad." (p. 49) However, Ruller's seeming conversion is still much blemished with vanity, so that his newly acquired faith is radically shaken when what he had sensed to be God's tokens of consideration and interest in him — the turkey placed in his way specially for him to take, or the beggar "God had gone out of His way to get" (p. 52) in order that he may give his alms — are yanked out of his hands. Terrified, panting with emotion as he slowly realizes that a bad trick has been played on him, his too hasty conviction that he and God were to be friends changes suddenly into a growing fear of "Something Awful . . . tearing behind him with its arms rigid and its fingers ready to clutch." (p. 53) What Ruller has come to understand is the fact that one does not make a deal with God, whose will and decisions are unquestionable and do indeed lie beyond the grasp of human beings. By the end of the story, the reader is sure that Ruller is on his way to humility, and that the part in himself which had been only halfheartedly listening has finally heard the mysteriously powerful voice of God inviting him to mend his ways.

A similar experience is the one young Harry Ashfield undergoes in "The River"; only his case is one of mere initiation. However craftily Flannery O'Connor plays on the double entendre of situations and events, toying with a symbolic level of reading of her tale, the boy's death remains questionable as a proof of real conversion, if only because of his tender age — he is only four or five; but it is possible at the conclusion of the tale to consider that the child is on his way to meet something divine. The setting of the story is laid out in terms of the child's perception. His universe is divided in two: on the one hand, his parents' flat where everything is a joke, in which he passes unnoticed and uncared for, where the roots of life get lost in the havoc caused by alcohol; and on the other hand, a recently envisioned new world, called the Kingdom of Christ, a world devoid of pain, promising happiness, in which, for the first time in his life, he may count. We know from the beginning of the story that Harry is going to live an important event, because of his very first words to Mrs. Connin's questions: he claims to be called Bevel, like the preacher they will see at the river, and he asks whether he will be healed. We may already consider that he has recognized what the preacher stands for, if only unconsciously. The story unfolds to tell the progression of Harry's awareness of the existence of Jesus Christ who created him, first with a picture "of a man wearing a white sheet . . . [with] long hair and a gold circle around his head," (p. 161) then with a little book recalling His life that he manages to steal and hide in the innerlining of his coat, and finally during his encounter with His spokesman on earth, the preacher who has come to speak His word. We also notice the boy's impatience to meet the preacher. But mostly, we register the unshakable determination which leads him back to the river. We know that the boy is seeking something, although we cannot be convinced that the realm of God which he has glimpsed during the healing session at the river bears for him the religious meaning intended by the preacher. Nevertheless, he returns quite determined, if not in search of the Holy in the strict sense of the term, at least in flight from a secular world in which he does not fit, for he is confident that this "River of Life", this "River of Love," as the preacher describes it, will lead him to happiness. O'Connor plays on that aspect of children's psychology which has them confuse the cryptic, symbolic words of grown-ups with their literal representation. In addition, Harry, combining the spontaneity, naïveté and imagination of his age, determines to settle alone matters which the adults around him refuse to explain. Hence his decision "to Baptize himself and to keep on going this time until he found the Kingdom of Christ in the river" (p. 173) as the result of an obstinate desire for recognition, because of the preacher's seductive assertion after baptizing him that he "count[s] now . . . [while he] didn't even count before." (p. 168) Bevel, as he has been calling himself throughout, en route to a world he knows intuitively to be fairer than the secular world of his parents, *is* nonetheless en route to the Kingdom of Christ as his young mind understands it, ineluctably drawn to a new life and to Jesus whom he does not know yet, but who he trusts will care for him. These elements allow us to accept O'Connor's conclusion of her tale, so that even though we may not interpret the boy's drowning as a true conversion, we can still generally adhere to the story for, as Martha Stephens explains:

> One reason why many of the individual stories are more successful than the novels is that O'Connor's formidable, often unreasonable doctrine about human life is generally not pushed in any one story beyond the bounds of common sense.[5]

"A Temple of the Holy Ghost" introduces a young girl of twelve whom several critics describe as an intriguing protagonist, and whom Martha Stephens goes so far as to suspect to be "the narrator of these bizarre tales herself."[6] In fact, this child appears to be one of the most mature among the young protagonists. Unlike the others, she exhibits a strikingly developed lucidity and a sense of God. Of course, like many other children, she is facetious, impudent, sullen, egotistical, slothful, "deliberately ugly to almost everybody" and "eaten up also with the sin of Pride, the worst one." (p. 243) But she is fully aware of a religiosity which affects her inner life and somehow troubles her. For instance, she is the only one to take seriously the meaning of Sister Perpetua's expression "I am a Temple of the Holy Ghost":

> She didn't see anything so funny in this. . . . I am a temple of the Holy Ghost, she said to herself, and was pleased with the phrase. It made her feel as if somebody had given her a present. (p. 238)

She also differentiates between the various Churches, despises Wendell and Cory who will become preachers of the Church of God, a function for which "you don't have to know nothing," (p. 239) and she is thankful that she herself does not belong to that Church. She is the only one to pray, even if occasionally, sometimes perfunctorily, but at times, and for no apparent reason, with fervor and delight. She has some knowledge of what saints and martyrs are, even fancies to become one. She is revolted when the two country boys mistake the *Tantum Ergo* for "Jew singing." The episode of the hermaphrodite recalled by her cousins puzzles her with the mystery of God's unfathomable will as well as with the mystery of the faith of the afflicted believer who unquestioningly accepts God's trials. Finally, on her visit to Mount St. Scholastica, she is taken to the chapel to hear the benediction and suddenly realizes that she is in the presence of God. She then starts praying humbly and sincerely. Again, the portrait Flannery O'Connor draws here is highly credible insofar as she mixes the two aspects of the child's universe: her secret, unexpressed, but pervasive religiosity, with the banality and absurdity of life around her which she mocks and criticizes. The girl is to sense and later to understand the dichotomy of life, comprised of the absurd material life on the one hand and of the meaningful spiritual life on the other.

In the story "The Lame Shall Enter First," we encounter an unusually amazing character, Rufus Johnson, a young fanatic so convinced that Satan has him in his power that he spends his life haunted by the devil while at the same time convinced of the truth of the Gospel and of the holiness of the Bible. In an act of violent sincerity, he proves his faith to atheist Sheppard by eating a page of the Book of Scriptures:

> Johnson swallowed what was in his mouth. His eyes widened as if a vision of splendor were opening up before him. "I've eaten it!" he breathed. "I've eaten it like Ezekiel and it was honey to my mouth!" . . . . "I've eaten it!" the boy cried. Wonder transformed his face. "I've eaten it like Ezekiel and I don't want none of your food after it nor no more ever." (p. 477)

In fact, the boy is fully conscious of his situation and opposes a fierce denial to every attempt of Sheppard to make him reason differently. From their very first meeting on, Rufus is the one to provide an explanation for his conduct. "I ain't asked for no explanation," he says; "I already know why I do what I do." (p. 450) With the same stubbornness, he affirms that he will go to hell, unless he repents and becomes a preacher, for there is no other end for the damned like him. He feels outraged in confronting Sheppard's belief that he can help and save him, because he is shocked to see that Sheppard is taking over God's prerogatives: "He thinks he's Jesus Christ!" (p. 459) the boy exclaims in a cracked voice, later retorting to stunned

Sheppard, "You ain't going to save me . . . Save yourself. . . . Nobody can save me but Jesus." (p. 474) Such fanaticism and violence in support of a religious conviction, as well as his malicious, ungrateful, vindictive behavior make Rufus a real demon himself and a frightening figure of a child. In the course of the story, we learn that Rufus's grandfather, who has gone to the hills to bury some Bibles in a cave and to reproduce Noah's ark, has had a decisive influence on the boy's convictions and creed, actually turning him into a religious freak. As Miles Orvell observes in his study, Rufus is one of those

> mad characters whose madness is born of frustration and anguish. Possessed by a sense of the vast importance of Redemption, or of a dream of salvation and paradise, [he is] yet unpossessed of grace. And [he] commit[s] acts of wanton violence . . . in accordance with [the] austere conviction of [his] sinful nature.[7]

At any rate, Rufus is the only one of Flannery O'Connor's children to be so totally lucid about his religious feelings and about the dimension of evil that lies within him and in the world around him. Torn between the two equally unfathomable powers of God and of Satan, he is at the same time prophet and demon, fearing the former and manipulated by the latter.

In these pages, we have shown how Flannery O'Connor endows her young characters with a consciousness of evil and an intensity of religious concerns, albeit at different levels. Even if we do not always take their violent gestures or appalling deaths for the manifestation of a forceful compulsion of faith burning inside of them, they convincingly show their ability to comprehend evil and good, to be morally responsible and spiritually sensitive, to respond to God's given signs, very much as adults can. However disturbing the fiendish twist to their personalities may be for the readers whose "gain in sensibility" usually corresponds to a "loss in vision,"[8] which Flannery O'Connor deplores, they should remember the author's oftentimes proclaimed standard:

> the writer whose vocation is fiction sees his obligation as being to the truth of what can happen in life, and not to the reader — not to the reader's taste, not to the reader's happiness, not even to the reader's morals.[9]

CHAPTER 3

CONCEITED, SELF-RIGHTEOUS CHRISTIANS

The collected stories as a whole present a recurrent pattern, which, as pointed out by several critics of O'Connor's works, reminds us of the life the author lived on her mother's farm in Milledgeville, Georgia, during her forced isolation. Several stories introduce energetic farm women who are struggling to try to maintain their place as a decent one through hard work and righteousness, while having to cope with both white and black hired help. In almost every case, they also have to support grown-up, hostile children who show no concern whatsoever for what is their mother's courageous travail. Mrs. Cope in "A Circle in the Fire," Mrs. Hopewell in "Good Country People," Mrs. May in "Greenleaf," Ruby Turpin in "Revelation," and Mrs. McIntyre in "The Displaced Person," all have in common the characteristics of self-righteous people. They take pride in whatever material security they have attained and hold in contempt everyone who has not succeeded in arriving where they have. In their self-satisfaction, they have forgotten about God and do indeed belong to that category of people which Flannery O'Connor alludes to when she declares:

> There is one type of modern man who recognizes spirit in himself but who fails to recognize a being outside himself whom he can adore as Creator and Lord; consequently he has become his own ultimate concern. . . . For him, man has his own natural spirit of courage and dignity and pride and must consider it a point of honor to be satisfied with this.[1]

In the course of the different stories, their reassuring self-image, as well as the tiny world these characters have come to master perfectly, will gradually be shaken. Ultimately, some unmistakable sign of God will cause the scales to be removed from their eyes, precipitating a moment of choice for them before their final collapse.

Except for Ruby Turpin, whose good disposition and successful marriage to Claud make her somehow slightly different from the others, all these women are widows who have taken over the charge of a farm and a family, painstakingly working their way through difficulties with steadfastness and decency in order to keep up their social position. Alert, industrious, organized, shrewd, efficient, business-like, they keep a sharp eye on everything. They believe that they are indispensable and like to repeat that they can see to and solve anything. Mrs. Cope's patronymic humorously alludes to this belief. Basking in a tranquilized contemplation of the possessions they have justly earned, these "self-intoxicated"[2] women count their blessings and perfunctorily address prayers of thanksgiving to God while urging everybody around them to do the same. Only, for the most part, they encounter incredulity. In tune with their universe, limited in scope to the gates surrounding their property, their mind and views of the world are also very much limited, and their self-expression constricted to a set of cliché-ridden apothegms they utter like so many parts of a litany. The banality of their thoughts as well as the smugness of their speech is what invariably infuriates their smarter daughters and sons trapped inside the confinement of their mothers' worlds because of some infirmity or other. The perception these women have of the world does not penetrate beyond the outward appearance, but they always speak out their genuine ignorance with a candid politeness which renders their family and friends impotent. Facts which they cannot exactly imagine, such as the gassing and deportation of Europeans during World War II, take in their mind a comical dimension, one which uses farm imagery, as more often than not they envision the poor souls "ridden in boxcars like cattle;" (p. 190) at the same time, such horrible events enable them to boast all the more of their own humanism and Christian behavior. The strength of character which has helped them reach a certain station in life, the hard work they have never refused, the high sense of decency they have never let weaken, a firm conviction that they know "who they are," all have converged to forge a clear-cut division of their society into two groups: on the one hand, the farm and land owners to which they belong; on the other hand, the white-trash, Negroes, or good-for-nothing hired help they have to confront. However, for all their apparent security, their optimism and their dogged propensity to see exclusively the good side of things, these Philistines are anxious, as we are given to discover little by little through the different stories. They are grateful for what they possess, but they live in constant dread of a catastrophe, and they cast suspicious glances at everybody around as if they were potential enemies plotting to crush them: the Negro hands are irresponsible; the white help are too slow, or they are careless enough to smoke while working; besides, they take no initiative and they would easily mistake one seed for another if not constantly watched after. In other words, these women see themselves as martyrs or victims, all the more so when, not only human beings but nature as well seem to be evils "sent directly by the devil to destroy their place." (p. 175) So that when an unexpected intruder comes about and, little by little, disturbs the order of the place, ending up wrenching the ground of success from under their feet, thus revealing their vulnerability, these naïve farm women inevitably collapse under the merciless *coup de grâce*. Powell and his two friends ("A Circle in the Fire"), efficient Mr. Guizac ("The Displaced Person"), the Greenleaf bull — symbolic of the entire Greenleaf family ("Greenleaf"), all precipitate the fall of these conceited women who subsequently realize that they had been mistaken in believing that they could hold their fate in their own two hands. In the course of each story, the menacing cloud they felt hovering over their head all along has finally burst open, pouring out its disaster, blurring all notions, shaking all certainties. Such a moment is highly decisive, insofar as the shock it has provoked is so great that it forces these self-righteous characters to confront human incompleteness and mortality, as well as the fragility of all worldly successes and earthly achievements. At the same time, when they recognize such facts, they also admit the mystery of God's creations. This is what Flannery O'Connor implies in essays about her fiction when she writes:

> There is a moment in every great story in which the presence of grace can be felt as it waits to be accepted or rejected . . . I have discovered that what is needed is an action that is totally unexpected, yet totally believable, and I have found that, for me, this is always an action which indicates that grace has been offered.[3]

While most of these women, when thus suddenly shaken, recover at once a notion of what humility is, Ruby Turpin ("Revelation"), who feels that she has grotesquely been accused of being "an old wart hog from hell" (p. 505) and therefore vehemently refuses the revelation, turns first her wrath against God in a hysterical verbal attack, challenging him with an outraged "Who do you think you are?" (p. 507) before the final vision overcomes her fury and leaves her humbly aware of her insignificance and dependence. In the course of each story, witnessing the progressive disintegration of their "self-made" worlds, until the final violent shock, these women are made to understand that all earthly matters are to be held in contempt and that man is indeed insignificant.

Ironically enough, in the stories mentioned, the white tenants show as much conceit and self-righteousness as their female bosses. It is the only way for them to express the superiority they feel over their colored counterparts, the Negroes who, in their eyes too, represent the bottom of society. At the same time, it allows them to vehemently deny an inferiority to their employers for the mere reason that they do not have any material possessions to their name: they may not be fortunate enough to run their own farm, but they pride themselves — and see to it that their masters realize it too — on being decent people and hard-working, reliable Christians. Again, in most cases, it is the wife in the tenant couples who is the dominating figure and the polite, but insistent, mouthpiece: Mrs. Shortley ("The Displaced Person"), Mrs. Pritchard ("A Circle in the Fire"), and Mrs. Freeman ("Good Country People") form a trio that Mr. Greenleaf is far from equaling in wit or sagacity. All three have vulgar characteristics: unlike their well-disposed, somewhat superstitious landladies who try to deny calamity by ignoring it, they make an avocation of it, even morbidly collecting newspaper clippings relating the details of secret infections, assaults upon children, incurable diseases and other such catastrophes. This seems to be essential to their daily equilibrium. They also seize every opportunity to enhance their own qualities and integrity by slyly alluding to other hired hands' misdeeds, without ever overtly denouncing anyone. Most of all, they take pleasure in casting panic in their fearful landladies' minds by forecasting all kinds of miseries that would ineluctably destroy the places kept up with so much pain and effort.

Whenever they can, the hired help point out advantages they seem to have acquired that their landladies have not: Mr. Greenleaf constantly refers to the success of his two sons while openly expressing his contempt for Mrs. May's own boys. Mrs. Freeman's daughters are two pleasant young girls who will marry nice young men while Joy — Mrs. Hopewell's daughter — never will because of her sullen temper, disgraceful face and nasty behavior. In other words, these characters try to compensate for their inferior rank in society and lack of possessions or material security in life by unsettling their well-provided for employers with the only weapon they have: insidious speech which will eventually precipitate their landladies to their fall. Unlike the latter, however, they generally do not experience any religious enlightenment when the catastrophes they had predicted happen; on the contrary, they remain the satisfied witnesses of collapses they feel to have justly smoothed away the unfair differences which existed between themselves and their social superiors. Except for Mrs. Shortley, whose character Flannery O'Connor has chosen to develop so as to make her realize, through a sudden climactic vision, the insignificance and emptiness of any human being and the nature of Christ's mercy, all the others are left in their initial ignorance as to what the mystery of God's creation really is.

The farm owners and their white tenants are not the only type of self-righteous Christians that Flannery O'Connor depicts in her fiction. Another set is represented by the grandmother of the story "A Good Man Is Hard to Find," and by Julian's mother in "Everything That Rises Must Converge." The two ladies can be compared insofar as they both incarnate the nostalgic figures of lost and longed for gentility. Both are somewhat pathetic because they have to accept and cope with a world which has become foreign to them. They make constant references to the time of their youth when good manners existed, when people had a strong sense of their identity, when the whites were the masters and the blacks their slaves by right. In embellished proportions, they provide endless descriptions of mansions and properties they once lived in or simply admired. They lament the fact that notions such as respect or decency have lost their true meaning. In their memories, they carry the cherished dream of life in days gone by forever and remain unadapted to their present environment. They behave in every way as if the disruption caused inside the universe of their youth had forever prevented them from growing up, and they display childish, irresponsible attitudes before the incensed members of their respective families. Their naïveté is disarming indeed, and despite the desperate efforts of their entourage, they cannot be made to realize that it does not fit but makes them all the more ridiculous in a world the values of which have considerably changed. Both women are convinced that they are respectable ladies and that they can be recognized as such by other people. But both fail to understand that the term is an empty one for their peers. When the grandmother, clad from head to foot in what she imagines to be the proper attire for a lady, clings desperately to that image of herself she figures will impress the Misfit, hysterically pleading "I know you wouldn't shoot a lady!" (p. 132) she is grossly unaware of the fact that the Misfit and she do not speak the same language. Similarly, when Julian's mother, digging out the brightest penny from her purse to offer it to the little Negro boy she has befriended in the bus is all of a sudden violently struck by the boy's outraged mother, the shock is so great, the denial of her genuine gift so unexpected, that her integrity is given a final blow from which she will not recover. These women are the victims of their own imagination, sentimentalism and outdated ideals. For all their xenophobia, condescension, and obsolete notions of class hierarchy, they are nonetheless sympathetic characters whose very ridiculousness arouses the reader's amused pity. Nevertheless, their vision of life is so limited, their concerns are so banal, their reactions so elementary, that the blow dealt to them when they are finally made to comprehend reality is necessarily fatal. Their cosy world is irremediably sinking, pulling them along in the destructive vortex which forever annihilates the cogency of their old inaccessible culture, while the immediacy of the new culture, if highly undesirable, bursts out in its derisive fullness. When they die, they have been made to envision the inadequacy of their selves, even if they are not ready to accept such condemnation.

The male counterpart of this group of self-righteous females is Mr. Head, the protagonist of "The Artificial Nigger," whose name aptly and humorously alludes to the many blemishes of his character. His pride lies in his conviction that age has given him a certain superiority and wisdom, and that he has achieved "that calm understanding of life that makes him a suitable guide for the young." (p. 249) He and his grandson Nelson constantly quarrel to demonstrate their ability to understand and settle issues. When the story opens, we learn that Mr. Head and Nelson are to make a trip to the city Nelson claims to know already since he was born there, a belief which Mr. Head hopes to weaken by showing his indispensability as a guide and by demonstrating his own sound experience when it comes to urban matters. Irritated by the boy's vanity, he has decided to humble him once and for all. He is fully confident in his knowledge of life and of the world. His iron will and strong character guide his moral and physical actions, and he is first described as having the composure and wisdom of "one of the great guides of men." (p. 250) Along the journey, not only Nelson, but Mr. Head too will come to realize the vulnerability of all men on earth and to acquire humility. The Christian experience Mr. Head still lacks but will undergo in the course of the story is foreshadowed in the opening scene of the tale when he wakes up to the smell of fatback Nelson is frying for breakfast, having thus disproved his grandfather's certainty that he must be first in all things; from then on, the readers are aware that Mr. Head's self-assurance has received the first of a long series of upsets they suspect will lead to his conversion. With every new incident occurring in the city, Mr. Head's authority and pride become more and more damaged in his grandson's eyes, then gradually in his own. There is an increasing intensity of nervousness and anxiety which builds up through the misadventures of the old man and the boy as they first lose their way, ending up in a black neighborhood and being compelled to ask a large Negro woman for directions, then as they are threatened with being reported to the police by a group of hysterical women who claim that Nelson has injured one of them. Unable to overcome his emotion and terror at such a prospect, Mr. Head denies having ever seen the boy, who is desperately clinging to him for help and security. This treachery is the first climactic moment of the tale as the old man, having cut himself off from the only being he loves and cares for, is left, facing disgrace and loneliness, to repent bitterly for the denial of his grandson, who has become a cold, mute, indifferent figure after the traumatic incident. Broken with shame and remorse, Mr. Head cries out his confession as he stops a passerby for help, uttering the symbolic words: "I'm lost! . . . Oh Gawd I'm lost! Oh hep me Gawd I'm lost!" (p. 267) Later, in the midst of despair, a second climactic moment occurs when the two wanderers come upon a plaster lawn figure of a Negro, which eventually serves as the instrument of their reconciliation as they stand "gazing at the artificial Negro as if they were faced with some great mystery, some monument to another's victory that brought them together in their common defeat." (p. 269) At this moment, both experience what mercy is, and Mr. Head is brought to understand the meaning of the word "sin," and to realize God's gracious Will to love and to forgive. The prideful guide has become a humble servant of God, one conscious of his insignificance, ready to enter Paradise.

Under the cover of comical situations, the stories mentioned in this chapter are constructed so as to demonstrate the sinful nature of human beings and the consequent necessity of God's grace and mercy. By the end of each story, the characters are given the opportunity to recognize God's sign, and thus to accept it or cast it aside. In most cases, their response is made clear for the reader; there are only a few of them whose reaction the author chooses to leave uncertain. The pattern of the tales, quite repetitive, is summed up by Carter W. Martin:

> Most of Flannery O'Connor's stories follow a pattern, the similarity of which arises largely from her invariably Christian perspective upon the characters and action. The pattern is that of the prototypical Christian experience, moving from the condition of sinfulness to a recognition of sin, repentance for it, confession, penance, and absolution.[4]

The truth that each character is offered is the revelation of God's redemption and of the divine nature of his immense forgiveness. Anybody humble enough to recognize his faults with sincerity and to repent for them may enter Paradise, after a supernatural experience has taken place. Flannery O'Connor's voice is prophetic of man's salvation when grace sanctifies his own otherwise futile efforts.

CHAPTER 4

INTELLECTUALS AND WOULD-BE ARTISTS

Flannery O'Connor's skillful use of deft and chilling irony is best demonstrated in her characterization of intellectuals and would-be artists. In five of her stories, she introduces bachelors and spinsters in their thirties who live the agony of being fully dependent on mothers whose values and petty concerns they loathe, mothers whom they can neither love nor leave, mothers because of whom they have turned into angry, isolated, impotent individuals. These smarter, frustrated individuals are trapped in a conflicting situation in which they see themselves as victims. However, as the author craftily shows, in reality they are all failures, ineffectual creatures who have deluded themselves in thinking that they know something, possess something, or can achieve something. The full irony of their situation lies in the fact that they blame their mother or their entourage for what they have become, while the core of their frustration rests in their ego. Hating the life they have to live, scorning their families, they have for the most part never made a move to escape; when they have, it was only to discover their inability to manage by themselves. Riveted to their mothers because of a weakness of body or of character, which renders them all the more furious, they turn to a world of pretense in which they suffer their martyrdom while shutting out everything that they find unbearable around them. Invariably, their ivory towers prove to be equally vulnerable shelters: in climactic instances in which they are given to realize their uselessness and ridiculousness, their fragile worlds collapse, living them aghast, compelled to confront reality. In each tale, the youths' illusive quest for values, their artistic humanism, or their deceitful identities are suddenly annihilated, and they must accept what their true nature really is, something which they have been denying all along.

Joy Hopewell, in "Good Country People," is the perfect stereotype of the intellectual. At thirty-two, she has hardly allowed herself much fun and pleasure. Highly educated, holding a Ph.D. in philosophy, she spends her time reading or retreated in her thoughts in order to avoid her mother's affable but commonplace and mediocre conversation; she tolerates other people around only for the sake of being spared the drudgery of having to pace the farm with her mother, for she dislikes nature anyway and hates anything related to it. She cannot help being rude to everybody because of the smugness and vanity she senses in people. She has never approached young men whom she finds invariably stupid; besides, she is all mind and cannot imagine herself touched by the matters of the heart. Through the years, she has managed to make herself the personification of hatred: endowed with a sullen disposition, she has a naturally ungracious appearance which she will not even try to improve with a smile; she has a wooden leg which she stomps heavily to make it more blatant; to round off the ugliness of her character, she has legally changed her name to Hulga, one she feels best fits her on account of its ugly sound and the connotations attached to it. The rage which eats her encompasses everything, including herself, and, unable to see anything positive or pleasant in life, she wants at least to make sure people know the conclusion she has come to, even if she cannot succeed in imposing it on them. However, in the course of a few hours, this solid, fierce, knowledgeable, all-too-sure maiden is shocked into recognizing her own self-deception, a discovery ironically provoked by a simple, innocent-looking Bible salesman who tricks her ruthlessly. The blow dealt to her is subtly and progressively orchestrated. At first, with domineering superiority, she despises Manley Pointer whom she takes for a simple country boy fool enough to be concerned with the Scriptures, while she has declared herself an atheist long ago. But on seeing him to the gate, she lets herself be talked into a picnic for the morrow. At this point, readers' suspicion is aroused as to what may be the first sign of a weakness that will later prove to be fatal, all the more so that, part of the night, she dreams of seducing the young boy, and that she goes to their rendezvous with whatever touch of femininity a whiff of Vapex used for perfume may impart. Once they are together, the boy flatters her in a deceitfully childlike way, and she vainly believes that he admires her. His kisses are so sweet, so innocent, his speech so genuine, his manners so awkward, that with full lucidity, amused detachment, and a trace of pity, she considers him like a baby she fancies for an instant to educate, to enlighten, and to rid of his blindfolds in order to bring him to "a deeper understanding of life." (p. 284) All of a sudden, though, the embryonic romance turns into a sadistic scene in which Joy-Hulga, who has surrendered completely to the boy by permitting him to take off her wooden leg, and, by so doing, has abandoned her very being to his care, is cruelly flouted when out of a hollow bible he has been carrying in his suitcase he exhibits a flask of whiskey and a deck of obscene cards. Moreover, once he has disclosed his true nature to her, assuring her that selling Bibles does not necessarily imply believing in the Bible, he runs away with her wooden leg which, he says, will enlarge his collection of "interesting things" that includes "a woman's glass eye" (p. 291) among other things. Left alone in the full intensity of the blow she has been given, with the terrible revelation delivered to her: "[y]ou ain't so smart. I been believing in nothing ever since I was born!" (p. 291), Joy-Hulga slowly realizes that she has been violently wrenched from her fragile pedestal.

In Julian, the protagonist of "Everything That Rises Must Converge," Flannery O'Connor has drawn a devastating portrait of a young, white, liberal Southerner torn between his unavowed longing for a past era and the certainty that it was one of wrongdoing, all the while finding the new one as repugnant and as insufferable in its low moral, intellectual, aesthetical, and social dimensions. Desperately trying to distinguish himself from everything which he hates in the South, he turns his wild hostility towards his mother who openly carries all the clichés of speech and manners (as to racism or class distinction, for instance) that she and the majority of her peers have not yet overcome. Sensitive, educated, with a dubious future as writer in front of him — while ironically reduced to sell typewriters in the meantime — depressed because of what he must confront, Julian can only retreat into the protecting bubble of his mind where he is free to see and condemn, and where he feels safe from any external judgment. His idealized image of himself is nonetheless very much threatened by self-doubt and self-pity, two feelings which prevent him from engaging in any creative or even relevant action. Every one of his attempts to assert his desire for integration turns awkwardly flat or takes tinges of sentimentalism. Wanting to teach his mother a lesson, he imagines all kinds of situations in which she would be so shocked that she would finally learn from her fundamental errors. Scenarios rush through his mind, which include getting a Negro doctor to save her from a desperate illness, befriending respectable Negro lawyers or distinguished Negro professors, bringing home a Negro fiancée, or demonstrating as a sympathizer at a sit-in. His efforts are miserable attempts which fall short of expectation. For instance, during the bus ride, when he deliberately addresses the Negro who is sitting next to him with the mere intention of disturbing his mother, his gesture of liberalism has an adverse effect: it only seems an annoyance to the Negro since the light he has asked for is of no service because of the "No smoking" sign posted over the door — furthermore, he has quit smoking some months before, unable to afford it any longer. Ironically, to Julian's dismay, despite her condescension and racist feelings for the entire Black race, it is his mother who succeeds in establishing a friendly contact with a little Negro boy, playing hide-and-seek with him through her fingers. In Julian's case, the pathos of his situation lies in the fact that he has genuinely convinced himself that he is emotionally free from his mother, that he can judge her with superior objectivity, that he is in no way dominated by her. It is all too obvious that these are only illusions. As a matter of fact, he is kept ineffectual and paralyzed by his unavowed emotional as well as physical dependence on her. Thus his life is a hopeless struggle against his confused feelings of guilt and frustration, of love for his mother and hatred for what she represents, of apparent detachment from human contacts and domination by them. In the final scene of the story, not only his mother, but he, too, learns his lesson. Rejoicing that she should at last realize facts in their blatant reality, ready to provide her with an explanation of their meaning, Julian's triumph is but very short: as his mother collapses to her death on the pavement, he suddenly comprehends the full horror of his own new and complete isolation, his tragic abandonment into a world hostile to him, a world highly detestable in which he now will necessarily meet his own symbolical death in the form of his innate inarticulateness and useless, albeit remorseful grief.

"The Enduring Chill" is a story which presents the progression of the inner crisis a young intellectual is undergoing just before his death which he thinks imminent, and the anticlimactic moment of revelation which suddenly destroys the sentimental world of illusions and sufferings he has created for himself when he realizes that he is not to die yet. Like every other young intellectual protagonist portrayed by Flannery O'Connor, Asbury is ill-tempered, sullen, egotistical, verbally aggressive, rude, spiteful, and highly disappointed in a family whose members he finds banal, stupid, and narrow-minded. Smarter and shrewder, he also has an artistic temperament and a liberal mind which make it all the more difficult for him to cope with and to accept the coarseness he witnesses around him. Despising his rural background, he has gone to New York, convinced that he could meet true culture there as well as enlightened minds to converse with. Soon, seriously ill, out of job and penniless, he is forced to come back to the family farm in the South to wait for his death, which he presumes to be close, but which will at least put an end to the moral agony he is sure to have to endure in the meantime. We learn that when he arrives, his self-assurance has just been dealt a serious blow, and that the false identity he has created upon assumed talents which he has progressively been obliged to recognize as illusory is taking blurred contours. The caustic prediction of his pragmatic sister that "Asbury can't write so he gets sick. He's going to be an invalid instead of an artist . . . all he's going to be around here for the next fifty years is a decoration" (p. 373) is indeed a true one, which Asbury tries in vain to ignore or refute, but which he faces more and more acutely every day. Unable to write or to create anything, he violently puts the blame on his mother, vehemently accusing her of a pernicious influence which turned him into the failure he is. The discovery of his shortcomings is a painful one indeed. Unable to unleash his despair openly to his mother, though, he has written her a long letter which he hopes will make her realize what part she had to play in his tragedy:

> I came here [New York] to escape the slave's atmosphere of home, . . . to find freedom, to liberate my imagination, to take it like a hawk from its cage and set it "whirling off into the widening gyre" (Yeats) and what did I find? It was incapable of flight. It was some bird you had domesticated, sitting huffy in its pen, refusing to come out! . . . . I have no imagination. I have no talent. I can't create. I have nothing but the desire for these things. Why didn't you kill that too? Woman, why did you pinion me? (p. 364)

Like Julian's, Asbury's feelings are of a conflicting nature. He feels scorn for his mother's vapidity, impatience for her maternal care which he finds excessive, hatred for her ego which he believes is destroying him, contempt for her lack of liberalism, self-loathing for his dependence on her, and a global devastating rage for everything that concerns her from far or near. Despite his obsessing fury, however, he is left paralyzed, with his wrath burning inside him, because of some mysterious bond which prevents him from ever attacking her directly. The conflict is entirely kept within the confines of his mind, as this is the only way he can pour forth bitter invectives against her. Only after his death will she discover the details of his living agony spelled out in the letter left for her. In reality, Asbury's ego, not his mother, is the sole instrument of his destruction. He is a failure in whatever he tries, for his convictions are inadequate, but instead of searching himself for the reasons of that inadequacy, he sees himself as the sad victim of an order around him that has gone entirely wrong. The point of self-recognition is close, though; a first hint is given when, upon his arrival on the farm, he crosses the dull gaze of a cow "watching him steadily as if she sensed some bond between them;" (p. 362) later, in a dream in which he visualizes his impending burial, with Art come to pay him his due tribute, he awakes with a shudder at the image of a "large white [cow], violently spotted, . . . softly licking his head as if it were a block of salt." (p. 374) In addition, Asbury's ultimate attempt to experience a last "moment of communion when the difference between black and white is absorbed into nothing" (p. 368) and racism completely annihilated, turns into a miserable failure and proves once and for all that communication with the black hired help on the farm is impossible. Furthermore, Father Finn, a Jesuit he has asked over to have a last intellectual talk before his death, proves to be different from the person he expected: unconcerned with literature, he is obsessed with prayers and catechism and delivers an accusatory sentence: "The Holy Ghost will not come until you see yourself as you are — a lazy ignorant conceited youth!" (p. 377) Ironically, the last stroke which crowns this series of steps towards lucidity is given him by his mother and Block, the family doctor, the two persons whose common sense and practical qualities he has been despising throughout his life with superior distrust; in a humorous instant, when Block delivers his diagnosis of Asbury's illness, triumphantly assuring that "undulant fever [will] keep coming back but . . . won't kill [him]," comparing it with "Bang's in a cow," (p. 381) the youth is left panting and aghast at the sight of the bright intense smiling face of his mother and at the simultaneous collapse of all his illusions. We may suspect that the violent anticlimax, which sweeps away his fancies of a romantic death that would have delivered him from the misunderstanding of his family and pals, while unfolding his own real nature in front of him, makes him envision a new life, together with newly emerging values.

Calhoun, the protagonist of "The Partridge Festival" is another example, like Asbury, of a young adolescent who has deluded himself about his talents and has created a false identity for himself; despite many evidences to the contrary, he persists in believing that he is an artist, a sensitive nature full of humanism, and that he is the only one among the people he lives with to correctly interpret the different manifestations of human behavior as well as to understand the meaning of life. Like the other youths mentioned previously, he likes to think that he is free in his doings and judgments. To be able to devote a large part of his time to art in general and writing in particular, he spends every summer busily selling all kinds of things, thus making money to afford independence the other three seasons. The fact that he is extremely good at selling, that he genuinely enjoys doing it, that he has been given an achievement scroll for his performance as a salesman casts a slightly unpleasant shadow on his ego which he would like to envision totally detached from anything material, above all from all petty concerns. He resolutely refuses any trace of resemblance with his late great-uncle whom he holds in contempt for his practical turn of mind and his calculating, businesslike character. Instead, the boy creates a fanciful portrait of himself after the image of Singleton, a murderer whose photograph in the newspaper has fevered his imagination. To him, Singleton is a victim of society to whom he is determined to do justice by writing a novel in which he will denounce the cruelty of the social system responsible for the man's sufferings and tragedy. Imbued with notions such as individualism, non-conformism, depth of character, and intellectual superiority, he walks the festive streets of the town where the shooting has taken place, trying in vain to collect manifestations of the townspeople's sympathy for Singleton, trying with equal uselessness to impose his own perception of him on the resentful inhabitants. However, such blatantly unanimous animosity on their part does not succeed in shaking his opposite convictions. Prompted by the girl next door whose sense of justice has been similarly injured by the whole case, he sets out with her to the State Hospital to confront the object of his artistic and humanistic delirium. Just before Singleton is introduced to them, Calhoun and Mary Elizabeth, whose hostility and scorn for one another have been high up to this point in the story, feel a sudden kinship overflow them in anticipation of the importance of the revelation that awaits them. The revelation proves to be important indeed, but hardly of the nature they expected. In front of them appears a hideous, gesticulating character who casts leering glances at the girl and utters suggestive remarks to her. The encounter does much to provide the two youths with an unequivocal representation of Singleton's true nature. Shocked by the frightening show, with their illusions and ideals suddenly destroyed, they understand the full extent of their initial error. Back on the road, exhausted after so intense an emotion, Calhoun pulls the car up the side of the highway; the sight of the reflection of his face in Mary Elizabeth's glasses precipitates his self-recognition: it is not an artist, but the master salesman he has always been who looks back at him triumphantly.

As is to be expected, the portrayal of these intellectuals and would-be artists is not gratuitous. For all the irony which shrouds it, O'Connor's point is clear: idealizing their own selves, creating fallacious identities which they praise, blinding themselves with the conviction of their superiority over their fellow men, adoring secular gods, such as Art, these heathen are on the wrong path because they see themselves as the center of a universe they interpret with erroneous values. They do satisfy Josephine Hendin's characterization of Flannery O'Connor's protagonists, whom she perceives as follows:

> Demanding neither hope nor salvation, O'Connor's heroes need only certainty. And all they can know absolutely, "know for sure," is isolation, rage, and death.[1]

Self-imposed, indeed, because self-created, isolation is their lot; a rage devastates them; and a symbolical death — the death of their old ego — awaits them and strikes them in an intense moment of enlightenment regarding their real nature, which turns out to be common rather than unique. The author's treatment of this type of character is different from her treatment of other types: their encounter with God or their sudden awareness of the universe in religious terms is not a direct one. Instead of learning about the presence and power of God, thus realizing the insignificance of human beings before the Divine, they discover the pettiness of their character, their vanity, their arrogance and their smugness only in reference to their own self. Of course, in the process, they learn Christian behavior, gain Christian qualities, discover what humility, charity, and altruism are, and they will eventually understand what religious connotations and implications these notions carry. However, whereas the presence of God has been revealed to the children or to the conceited, self-righteous people we have dealt with previously, it is not immediately revealed to the intellectuals or would-be artists: they will first approach it, then will discover it only after a necessary trudging along the path of Christianity has taken place. Ultimately, though, they will learn the same lesson as other characters portrayed in the stories, and will be given the opportunity to discriminate between human nature, human matters, human vulnerability, human uncertainty, human damnation on earth, and supernatural, almighty Divinity. With this category of characters, O'Connor has pushed irony to the extreme, for she has chosen to create her intellectuals and would-be artists as declared atheists. Such a device, blatant as it may be, is nonetheless a powerful one.

CONCLUSION

Flannery O'Connor's fictional world may convince or may repulse, but it will certainly never leave indifferent. One of its most appealing qualities might very well be that strange combination of the comic and the pathetic, or that paradox which presents a fallen world in which there is hope. In her work, her innate comic spirit and her religious convictions are closely interwoven. It was her vision of the invisible which allowed her to see the comic aspect of life around her. In one of her essays, she wrote: "Only if we are secure in our beliefs can we see the comical side of the universe."[1] For her, man on earth is only a lonely clown, comical in his floundering but endearing in his efforts to recognize and accept his humility. Human nature being essentially sinful and weak, man cannot possibly manage without assistance. God provides his assistance to those who seek it, and however fallen the world as the author depicts it may appear, grace can operate, and redemption may be bestowed. Such a prophecy is the one O'Connor endlessly proclaimed in her tales. Her stories are stories of hope, for when the characters admit the existence of evil in themselves and in others, they are left to look into their hearts and souls, to consider their limitations and their imperfections, and to seek divine grace and mercy. Physical ugliness and suffering, horrible events, violent deaths should not distress the oversensitive reader; rather, they should be taken as evidence that something greater has been granted. Indeed, when it occurs, death almost invariably provides the characters' salvation — at least, it offers it, leaving it to the characters to accept or to reject it. In these delightfully comic but chillingly edifying short stories, Flannery O'Connor's doctrinal tone powerfully and unremittingly discloses that great mystery of life: the redeemability of every human creature.

ENDNOTES

Chapter 1

1. Flannery O'Connor, "The King of the Birds," *Mystery and Manners* (New York: Farrar, Straus & Giroux, 1969): 4.

2. Flannery O'Connor, "The Fiction Writer and His Country," *Mystery and Manners*: 32.

3. Flannery O'Connor, "Some Aspects of the Grotesque in Southern Fiction," *Mystery and Manners*: 43.

4. Flannery O'Connor, "The Church and the Fiction Writer," *Mystery and Manners*: 146.

5. Flannery O'Connor, "The Fiction Writer and His Country," *Mystery and Manners*: 34.

6. John Wakeman, ed., *World Authors: 1950-1970. A Companion Volume to Twentieth Century Authors*. (New York: The H.W. Wilson Company, 1975): 1078.

7. Flannery O'Connor, "The Church and the Fiction Writer," *Mystery and Manners*: 144.

8. Sister M. Bernetta Quinn, "Flannery O'Connor, a Realist of Distances," in Melvin J. Friedman and Lewis A. Lawson, eds., *The Added Dimension: The Art and Mind of Flannery O'Connor* (New York: Fordham University Press, 1966): 171.

9. Stanley E. Hyman, *Flannery O'Connor* (Minneapolis: University of Minnesota Press, 1966): 8.

10. Flannery O'Connor, "On Her Own Work," *Mystery and Manners*: 112.

11. Flannery O'Connor, "Novelist and Believer," *Mystery and Manners*: 162.

Chapter 2

1. Flannery O'Connor, "Introduction to *A Memoir of Mary Ann*," *Mystery and Manners*: 222.

2. Flannery O'Connor, "The Catholic Novelist in the Protestant South," *Mystery and Manners*: 209.

3. Sister Kathleen Feeley, *Flannery O'Connor: Voice of the Peacock* (New Brunswick: Rutgers University Press, 1972): 23.

4. Martha Stephens, *The Question of Flannery O'Connor* (Baton Rouge: Louisiana State University Press, 1973): 155.

5. Martha Stephens, *Ibid.*: 145.

6. Martha Stephens, *Ibid.*: 155.

7. Miles Orvell, *Invisible Parade: The Fiction of Flannery O'Connor* (Philadelphia: Temple University Press, 1972): 44.

8. Flannery O'Connor, "Introduction to *A Memoir of Mary Ann*," *Mystery and Manners*: 227.

9. Flannery O'Connor, "Catholic Novelists and Their Readers," *Mystery and Manners*: 172.

Chapter 3

1. Flannery O'Connor, "Novelist and Believer," *Mystery and Manners*: 159.

2. Stanley E. Hyman, *Flannery O'Connor* (Minneapolis: University of Minnesota Press, 1966): 36.

3. Flannery O'Connor, "On Her Own Work," *Mystery and Manners*: 118.

4. Carter W. Martin, *The True Country: Themes in the Fiction of Flannery O'Connor* (Nashville: Vanderbilt University Press, 1969): 104.

Chapter 4

1. Josephine Hendin, *The World of Flannery O'Connor* (Bloomington: Indiana University Press, 1970): 37.

Conclusion

1. Flannery O'Connor, "Novelist and Believer," *Mystery and Manners*: 167.

BIBLIOGRAPHY

1. Primary Sources

O'Connor, Flannery. *The Complete Stories*. New York: Farrar, Straus & Giroux, 1971.

____________________. *Mystery and Manners*. Occasional Prose, selected and edited by Sally and Robert Fitzgerald. New York: Farrar, Straus & Giroux, 1969.

2. Secondary Sources

Abbott, Louise H. "Remembering Flannery O'Connor." *Southern Literary Journal* 2, 2 (1970): 3-25.

Bassan, Maurice. "Flannery O'Connor's Way: Shock, with Moral Intent." *Renascence* 15, 4 (1963): 195-199, 211.

Brittain, Joan. "The Fictional Family of Flannery O'Connor." *Renascence* 19 (1966): 48-52.

Browning, Preston M., Jr. "Flannery O'Connor and The Demonic." *Modern Fiction Studies* 19 (1973): 29-41.

____________________. *Flannery O'Connor*. Carbondale and Edwardsville: Southern Illinois University Press, 1974.

Cheney, Brainard. "Miss O'Connor Creates Unusual Humor out of Ordinary Sin." *Sewanee Review* 71 (1963): 644-652.

Dowell, Bob. "The Moment of Grace in The Fiction of Flannery O'Connor." *College English* 27, 3 (1965): 235-239.

Drake, Robert. " 'The Bleeding Stinking Mad Shadow of Jesus' in The Fiction of Flannery O'Connor." *Comparative Literature Studies* 2 (1966): 183-196.

______________. "The Paradigm of Flannery O'Connor's True Country." *Studies in Short Fiction* 6 (1969): 433-442.

Driskell, Leon V. and Joan T. Brittain. *The Eternal Crossroad: The Art of Flannery O'Connor*. Lexington: University Press of Kentucky, 1971.

Eggenschwiler, David. *The Christian Humanism of Flannery O'Connor*. Detroit: Wayne State University Press, 1972.

Esprit 8 (Winter 1964).

Feeley, Kathleen. *Flannery O'Connor: Voice of The Peacock*. New Brunswick: Rutgers University Press, 1972.

Fickett, Harold and Douglas R. Gilbert. *Flannery O'Connor. Images of Grace*. Grand Rapids, MI: William B. Eerdmans Publishing Company, 1986.

Fitzgerald, Robert. Introduction to *Everything That Rises Must Converge*. New York: Farrar, Straus & Giroux, 1965.

Friedman, Melvin J. and Lewis A. Lawson, eds. *The Added Dimension: The Art and Mind of Flannery O'Connor*. New York: Fordham University Press, 1966.

__________________ and Beverly Lyon Clark, eds. *Critical Essays on Flannery O'Connor*. Boston: G.K. Hall & Co., 1985.

Gentry, Marshall Bruce. *Flannery O'Connor's Religion of the Grotesque*. Jackson: University Press of Mississippi, 1986.

Hart, Jane. "Strange Earth: The Stories of Flannery O'Connor." *Georgia Review* 12 (1958): 215-222.

Hendin, Josephine. *The World of Flannery O'Connor*. Bloomington: Indiana University Press, 1970.

Hyman, Stanley E. *Flannery O'Connor*. Minneapolis: University of Minnesota Press, 1966.

Kropf, C.R. "Themes and Setting in 'A Good Man Is Hard to Find.' " *Renascence* 24 (1972): 177-180, 206.

Martin, Carter W. *The True Country: Themes in the Fiction of Flannery O'Connor*. Nashville: Vanderbilt University Press, 1969.

May, John R. "The Pruning Word: Flannery O'Connor's Judgement of Intellectuals." *Southern Humanities Review* 4 (1970): 325-338.

McCarthy, John F. "Human Intelligence Versus Divine Truth: The Intellectual in Flannery O'Connor's Works." *English Journal* 55 (1966): 1143-1148.

McKenzie, Barbara. *Flannery O'Connor's Georgia.* Athens: University of Georgia Press, 1980.

Muller, Gilbert H. *Nightmares and Visions. Flannery O'Connor and the Catholic Grotesque.* Athens: University of Georgia Press, 1972.

Orvell, Miles. *Invisible Parade: The Fiction of Flannery O'Connor.* Philadelphia: Temple University Press, 1972.

Paulson, Suzanne Morrow. *Flannery O'Connor. A Study of the Short Fiction.* Boston: G.K. Hall, Twayne's Studies in Short Fiction Series No 2, 1988.

Quinn, Sister M. Bernetta. "View from a Rock: The Fiction of Flannery O'Connor and J.F. Powers." *Critique* 2 (1959): 19-27.

Sewanee Review 76 (1968): 261-356.

Shear, Walter. "Flannery O'Connor: Character and Characterization." *Renascence* 20 (1968): 140-146.

Stelzmann, Rainulf. "Shock and Orthodoxy: An Interpretation of Flannery O'Connor's Novels and Short Stories." *Xavier University Studies* 2 (1963): 4-21.

Stephens, Martha. *The Question of Flannery O'Connor.* Baton Rouge: Louisiana State University Press, 1973.

Taylor, Henry. "The Halt Shall Be Gathered Together: Physical Deformity in The Fiction of Flannery O'Connor." *Western Humanities Review* 22 (1968): 325-338.

Wakeman, John, ed. *World Authors: 1950-1970. A Companion Volume to Twentieth Century Authors.* New York: The H.W. Wilson Company, 1975.

www.ingramcontent.com/pod-product-compliance
Lightning Source LLC
Chambersburg PA
CBHW020943310726
48980CB00001B/31
9780761810407